LUCY LOU

Lucy Lou

Written By

Terry Sewell

&

Illustrated Artwork

Johno Cornish

DEDICATION

Thanks to Johno Cornish who inspired me by his influential art in creating this book.

Hopefully, children everywhere will enjoy its pages and unique illustrations:

Terry Sewell

They say that fairytales and dreams can never come true, but they can in a story.
One day you might become a writer too and make all your fairytales and dreams come true by simply using both the nib of a pen and a screwdriver, as in the tale of Lucy Lou.

Once upon a time,
lived a girl-
called Lucy Lou,

Tumble Down Farm,
is where she lived-
and grew.

One day Lucy got upset,
as the house-
had been sold,

without any breakfast,
she ran off-
into the cold.

Lucy sat beside a tree-
looking very sad,

wondered what was going on-
while feeling really mad.

Lucy thought-
about the good times,
with a teardrop-
in her eye,

playing hide and seek-
with brother Paul,
in special days-
gone by.

Lucy used-
to love to play,
on a bright-
and breezy day,

flying her kite-
up in the sky,
while her hair-
got blown away.

Tommy Huckle-
used to join her,
with his red kite too,

taught her how to fly-
a kite,
exactly what to do.

Once,
Tommy surprised Lucy-
at her favourite tree,

made her a swing-
to play on,
very happily.

Their special place-
they used to chat,
sat, by the old oak tree,

where they kissed-
for the first time,
Lucy Lou and Tommy.

She remembered other days-
along with brother Paul,

out by the orchard,
throwing Patch-
the dog his ball.

Visiting the lighthouse,

scoffing Ma Crumble's-
tea and cake,

but tomorrow–
it could all end,

according to the sign–
by the broken gate.

Lucy was unhappy-
so simply ran away,

no one would ever-
make her leave,
she was here to stay.

Meanwhile, Harry Hare-
and Dizzy Dragonfly,

sat chatting in a field-
as Lucy Lou ran by.

Hilda Hare spotted Lucy-
running away too,

but neither Hilda or Harry,
knew excactly-
what to do.

"Well, we must do something,
said Betty Butterfly,

we can't sit here-
doing nothing,
we've really got to try."

"Yes try we must,
said Bumble-Bee,
with his usual hum,

I'll keep a lookout for her,
so sorry-
I can't come."

Robin Redbreast whispered-
into Hilda Hares ear,

"Someone must help Lucy,
on her own out there."

Harry Hare-
sat to stare,
by the Tulips-
deep in thought,

worried Lucy Lou-
would get caught-
in the rain.

18

Wise Summer Sunflower,
told Harry-
what to do,

with a hop and a skip-
brave Harry,
chased after-
Lucy Lou.

Dark clouds gathered,
in an angry looking sky,

over Summer Sunflowers-
home patch,
looking scary to the eye.

20

Lucy Lou-
grew out of breath,
having reached-
the railway line,

crossing past Poppy Corner-
crying all the time.

So many things-
went through Lucy's mind,
like the harvest-
in the summer,

sat on the bales-
in the warm sunshine,
playing with her brother.

Right now she felt cold-
with black clouds ahead,

missing her home-
and her snugly warm bed.

Lucy knew-
that Tommy,
lived somewhere-
in the wood,

so went off-
to find him,
if only she could.

24

Luckily,
Lucy had her brolly-
at hand,

as the rain poured down-
on the soaked woodland.

Suddenly,
the wind-
blew her brolly away,

but at least-
she had her cape on,
to keep the rain at bay.

Lucy tripped surprisingly,
hit her head-
on a tree,

when she tried to get up-
found it hard to see.

Having lost her brolly-
her cape now too,

Harry Hare was on the way-
to rescue Lucy Lou.

Lucy felt tired,
fell into a sleep,

imagined walking in the snow-
which didn't seem too deep.

Then suddenly,
a spaceship-
appeared before her eyes,

about to land-
in front of her,
taking Lucy by surprise.

But in a blink of an eye,
the spaceship disappeared,

it was a low flying aeroplane-
which made poor lucy scared.

Lucy's last memory,
while struggling with her breath,

was seeing a man on the moon-
as she lay shivering to death.

Harry Hare reached the wood-
wondering which way to go,

but wasn't that sure-
as he didn't really know.

Harry asked-
Spike the hedgehog,
if he'd seen-
Lucy Lou,

but he replied sadly-
"No, I haven't got a clue."

In the awful storm,
Harry searched-
far and wide,

but was getting nowhere,
until a fairy-
appeared at his side.

" I am the fairy-
of all that is good,

here to help find Lucy-
somewhere in the wood.

"My magic dust,
will show you-
the way,

you must find her quickly-
that's all I can say."

The fairy's hand opened-
letting the magic dust go,

"Now follow it, Harry-
to the end of the rainbow,

there you will find-
your Lucy,

by the mysterious tree-
where the sky is blue."

Harry raced away-
with no time to spare,
following the magic dust-

until he found lucy there,
sat at the end of the rainbow-
by the mysterious tree,
smiling and waving-
happily.

"Oh, Harry-
she said,
I'm so lucky-
to be alive,

I nearly froze to death-
and don't know how I survived.

41

"But what happened-
to the snow?
where did it go?

"I don't know lucy-
Harry replied,
but we really must go."

Harry showed Lucy-
the track back home,

on the way-
he warned her,
not to go off alone.

Lucy said sorry-
she'd been so upset

as a balloon-
flew over poppy fields,
every flower-
soaking wet.

44

Lucy spoke to Harry-
about the things she'd miss.

like the man-
she bought balloons off,
as a young kid.

How she loved Yellow Wagtail-
chirping away,

to handsome Mr Cockerel-
early morning,
every day.

Walking in the field-
by a tiny winding stream,

where once-
she saw a red sun,
that almost seemed a dream.

The summer when the fields-
all turned yellow,

burnt by the sun-
in every single meadow.

The footbridge-
where she sat to watch,
the many trains-
go by,

the fields of crops-
forget-me-nots,
so pleasing to her eye.

The Scarecrow on fifty acres-
who as a child,
she thought was real,

how the crows loved him,
he had such-
an appeal.

Lucy often wandered-
up the maple straight,

to see-
the magic golden tree,
brightening up-
the whole estate.

The day when Mrs Peacock-
sat on the electric supply,

looking so beautiful-
with all her feathered eyes.

Suddenly on a motorbike-
Lucy's dad appeared,

after Hilda Hare-
had told him,
she was lost-
in the woods somewhere.

"Oh Lucy, thank goodness-
you are safe,

you scared me so much-
I'm in a right old state,

your mother is sick-
with worry,
after searching-
in the rain,

she will be so happy-
when I get you home again,

especially-
after PC Black,
caught your brother-
stealing sweets,

running out of the shop-
when he was on the beat."

Her dad Billy-
rode Lucy back home,
Harry had to follow-
because there was no room,

"By the way, said Billy,
why did you run away?"

"I thought you'd sold-
the farm dad,

there was a sign-
by the gate today."

Lucy stood shocked,
she could hardly-
believe her eyes,

the sign-
had completely vanished,
it was a huge surprise.

"We bought the farm silly,"
said Billy-
with a tear in his eye,

"Oh, dad-
that's so wonderful,"
Lucy Lou replied.

A week later-
they all went on holiday,

Lucy had a great time,
in each and every way,

yet,
she couldn't wait-
to get back to Tumble Down,

marry Tommy Huckle...
some day.

Later that same year,
Tommy asked her-
to be his bride,

Lucy said yes-
and they married,
both out of love-
and pride.

Lucy enjoyed-
her wedding,
along with her three-
best friends,

dancing all night together,
with Patch joining in-
at the end.

They both had-
a wonderful honeymoon,
stayed at a beautiful hotel,

in a room looking out-
to the seaside,
on the coast of the-
Costa Del Vell.

Once back home-
to Tumble Down,

the two settled together-
as one.

Later that year-
Lucy Lou now a Huckle,
gave birth to their first-
baby son,

and they all lived happily-
ever after,
each and every one-
of them.

We hope you enjoyed both the story written by Terry Sewell and illustrated by Johno Cornish artwork, hopefully they will publish another one together soon.

SCREWDRIVER ARTIST – JOHNO CORNISH

Johno Cornish is an Artist raised near the beautiful Norfolk Broads. His work is different, exciting and already very popular. It wasn't until a life changing experience in 2005, when he tried to take his own life, that he started painting as part of his recovery. He painted  sporadically with paint brushes but didn't like what he was producing. So, in 2017, he decided to experiment with painting with screwdrivers and gloss paint, and the experiment worked! Johno calls his work 'Art of the Soul' because everything comes from within and every painting tells a story.

Some of Johno's paintings are from his imagination and others from the photographs that he takes of his surroundings. He especially loves trees and hares, so many of his works focus on these two subjects.

Johno believes art is great therapy. He is now introducing his art into well-being workshops to help people with mental health issues. He believes that art saved his life and he wants to help others overcome their fears.

Johno is passionate about his art and is starting to live his dream working as a full-time artist.

Johno Cornish Mobile 07939 232797
Email: johnyfaith@gmail.com

 Johno Cornish    johnocornish_screwdriverartist

69

Johno Cornish
The Artist at work

a unique artist
using screwdriver techniques.

PUBLISHED AUTHOR/PRIZE-WINNING POET

Terry SEWELL

An accomplished published writer of both fiction and non-fictional works. He writes children's magical tales and adult-only thrillers. Terry also writes lyrics and short stories with a twist in the tale:

Number
07725476731

Email
terrysewelli@yahoo.co.uk

Facebook groups
https://www.facebook.com/groups/293860908755901
https://www.facebook.com/Terrysewellfictionauthor/

Twitter
https://twitter.com/te_author
Website:
https://tellataleterry4u.site123.me

LinkedIn
https://www.linkedin.com/in/terry-sewell-4488011b3/

Experience

Terry has been a serious published writer now for six years. He has been a guest on BBC Radio, and a frequent visitor to schools and colleges throughout East Anglia to both encourage and inspire students, through his own work and creative workshops within the written word .

His written works have already received good reviews and can be found by this link: https://www.amazon.co.uk/Terry-Sewell/e/B073HBG2XY?ref_=nav_signin&

Terry is always available for book signings, author talks, and an audience with the author afternoons/evenings. Plus workshops and guest appearances.

Comments About the author and his works: *Terry has been compared to E.E.Cummings the prolific American poet: His children's book The Battle of the Reds and the Greys have been compared to Water Ship Down by the great Richard Adams & his thriller Hurt, to Fifty-Shades of Grey.*

Terry Sewell at work on yet another story.

a gifted storyteller and prize-winning poet.

Johno's Facebook page can be found by pasting this link below. https://www.facebook.com/john o.cornish.

Terry's Facebook and website can be found by pasting these links:
https://www.facebook.com/Terrysewellfictionauthor/
https://app.site123.com/manager/wizard.php?w=897741&from=dash

Other Children's books
by the Author
Terry Sewell:

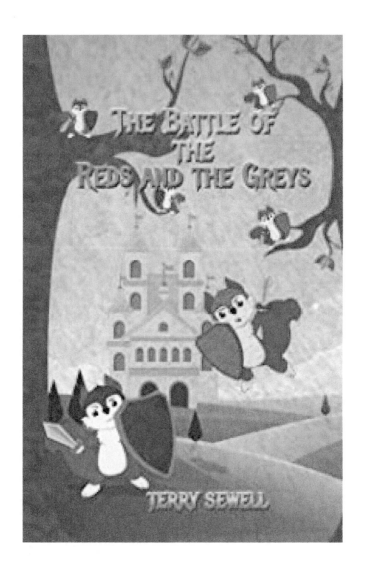

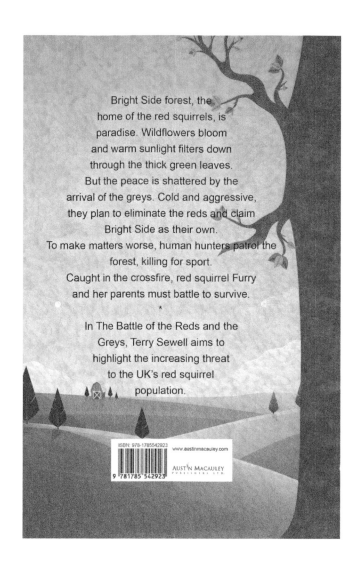

Bright Side forest, the
home of the red squirrels, is
paradise. Wildflowers bloom
and warm sunlight filters down
through the thick green leaves.
But the peace is shattered by the
arrival of the greys. Cold and aggressive,
they plan to eliminate the reds and claim
Bright Side as their own.
To make matters worse, human hunters patrol the
forest, killing for sport.
Caught in the crossfire, red squirrel Furry
and her parents must battle to survive.

*

In The Battle of the Reds and the
Greys, Terry Sewell aims to
highlight the increasing threat
to the UK's red squirrel
population.

ISBN: 978-1785542923   www.austinmacauley.com

AUSTIN MACAULEY
PUBLISHERS LTD.

9 781785 542923

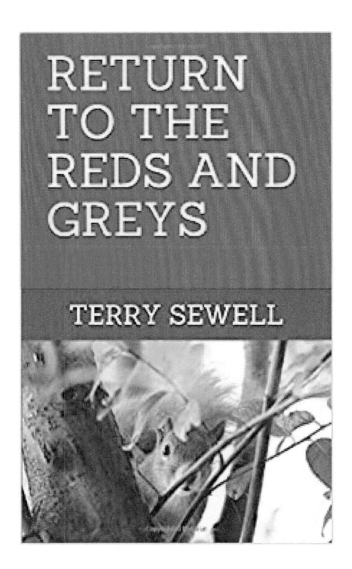

When Jill and John decide to build a Snowman, Jill goes one better by creating a Snowgirl. But when a magical fairy arrives on the scene to grant a wish John leaves Jill to it discounting her wishes to be false.

The tale of the Snowgirl came about by a dream, in fact, most of the author's children's stories were inspired by dreams. The author publishes both fiction short stories as well as poetic prose and rhyme. His latest book for adults only is a thriller having had some great reviews.

The author Terry Sewell has always wanted to write about a Snowgirl after being inspired by the great Raymond Briggs after having admired his picture book. Terry's books can be found on amazon.co.uk either in paperback or kindle only. He is available for book signings and author talks throughout both counties of East Anglia. He also has a website https://tellataleterry4u.site123.me Terry has three Facebook groups covering Norfolk and Suffolk. If you wish to join his fanbase you can request to be a member at...
https://www.facebook.com/groups/229999894710943

ISBN 9798580050553

90000

9 798580 050553

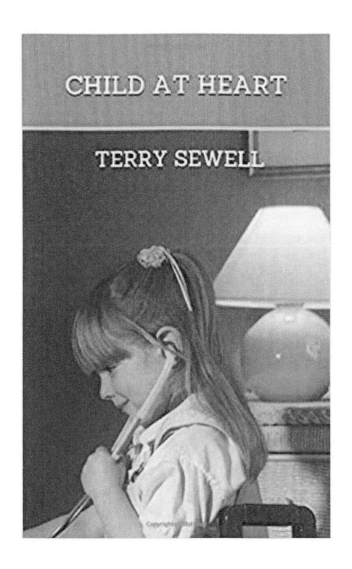

MAGICAL
CHILDREN'S
STORIES

TERRY SEWELL
TALES
FEATURING:

HOLLY CHRISTMAS
PENNY & POPPY PIGTAILS
THE TRUTH FAIRY
TREE OF MIRRORS
THE CHIMES OF ANGELS

ISBN 9781549873232

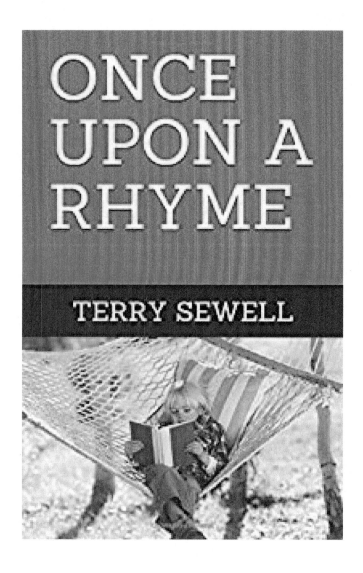

Terry's next children's book is entitled: Sammy Squirrel.

A charming tale of Sammy Squirrel growing up deep in the heart of Redwood Forest.

A not to be missed book, coming soon.

LUCY LOU

Printed in Great Britain
by Amazon

62384865R00058